Navajo ABC

A Diné Alphabet Book

written by **Luci Tapahonso** and **Eleanor Schick**
illustrations by **Eleanor Schick**

Simon & Schuster Books for Young Readers

Díí naaltsoos shisóóké bá 'iishłaa

Briana Nezbah Edmo dóó

Chamisa Bah Edmo.

L. T.

For Dr. Moheb S. Moneim,

who gave me back my drawing hand

E. S.

SIMON & SCHUSTER BOOKS FOR YOUNG READERS
An imprint of Simon & Schuster Children's Publishing Division
1230 Avenue of the Americas, New York, New York 10020

Text copyright © 1995 by Luci Tapahonso and Eleanor Schick
Illustrations copyright © 1995 by Eleanor Schick

All rights reserved including the right of
reproduction in whole or in part in any form.
SIMON & SCHUSTER BOOKS FOR YOUNG READERS is
a trademark of Simon & Schuster.
Book design by Carolyn Boschi
The text for this book is set in Palatino.
The illustrations are rendered in colored pencil on vellum over bristol.
Manufactured in the United States of America
First edition
10 9 8 7 6 5 4 3 2 1
LIBRARY OF CONGRESS CATALOGING-IN-PUBLICATION DATA
Tapahonso, Luci.
Navajo ABC: a Diné alphabet book / written by Luci Tapahonso and
Eleanor Schick: illustrations by Eleanor Schick.—1st ed.
p.   cm.
ISBN 0-689-80316-8
1. Navajo Indians—Juvenile literature.
2. Navajo language—Glossaries, vocabularies, etc.—Juvenile literature.
[1. Navajo Indians.   2. Alphabet.
3. Navajo language—Glossaries, vocabularies, etc.]
I. Tapahonso, Luci,   ill.   II. Title.
E99.N3S335 1995   497´.2—dc20   94-46881

Foreword

We call ourselves T'áá Diné, which means "The People." We are also called the Navajo. There are about 220,000 Diné today. Our land is in Utah, New Mexico, and Arizona. We speak the Diné language, and many of our schools teach children to read and write Diné, as well as English. Our language is very important; because of it we are able to remember and practice many of the old ways that our ancestors taught us.

We are happy to share some of our daily lives with our readers. All of the objects and words in this alphabet book are only parts of larger ideas, which are expressed through stories, songs, and prayers. Through these stories, songs, and prayers, we learn about animals and plants, we learn to respect one another, and we learn about the world around us. We also learn about our history, the land's history, and how to be responsible for the world we live in. The Diné language teaches us to be strong and have pride in all that we do.

Aa Arroyo

B b Belt

Cc Cradle board

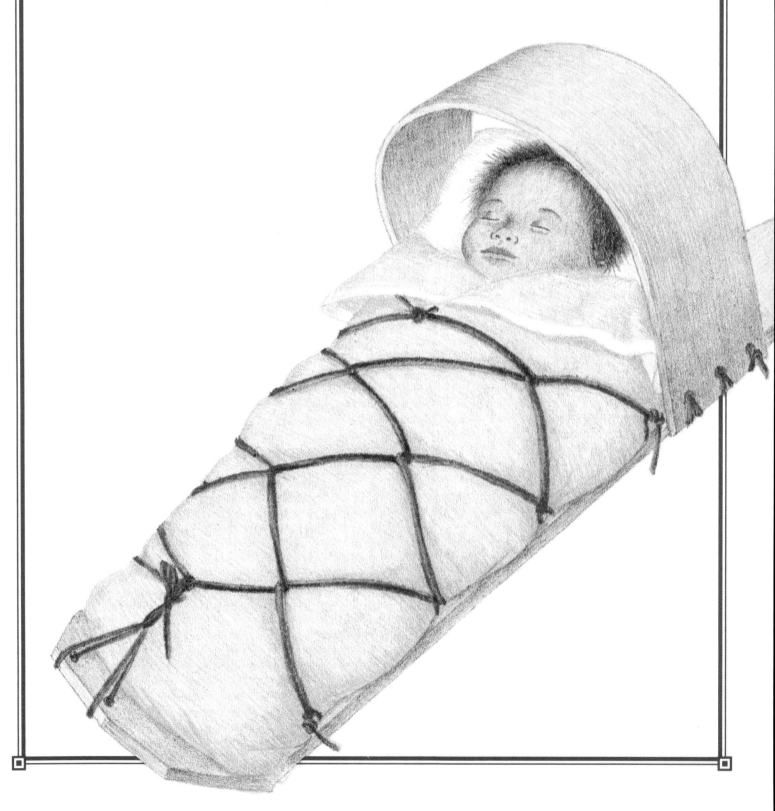

Dd Dress

Ee Earrings

Ff Fry bread

Gg Grandma

Hh Hooghan

Ii

'I'íí'ą́

Jj Juniper berries

Kk Kéyah

Ll Loom

Mm Moccasin

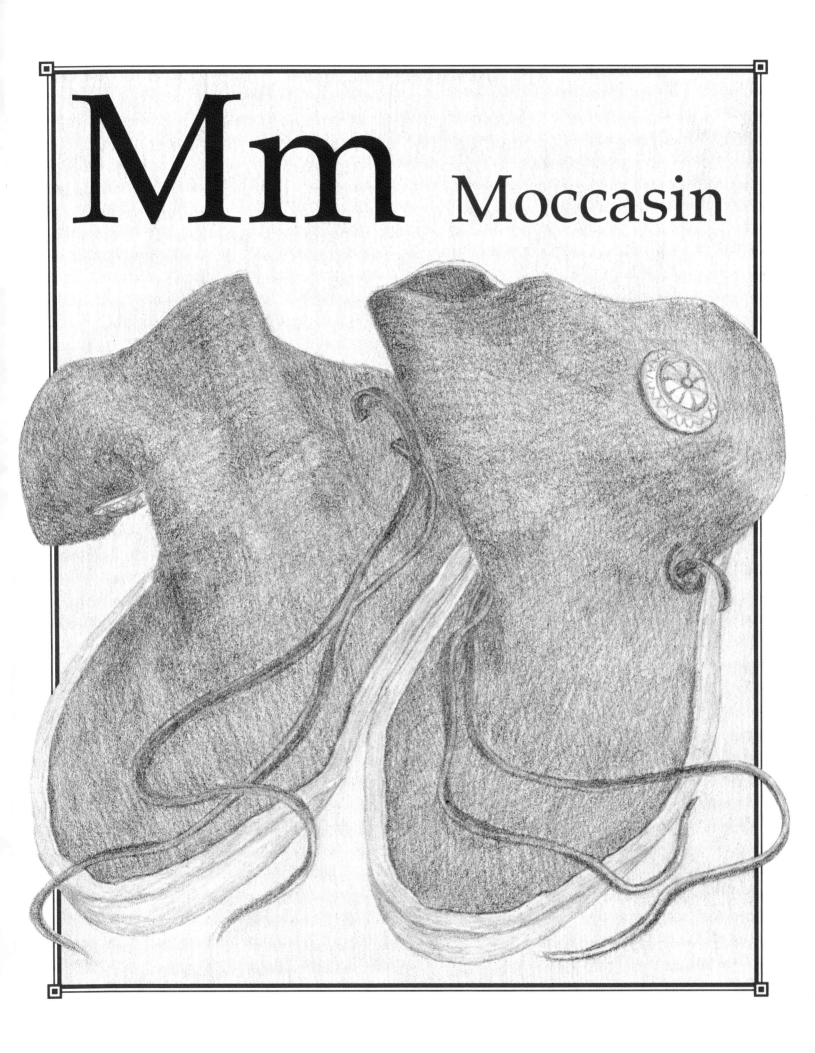

Nn Necklace

Oo 'Ooljéé'

Pp Pottery

Qq Quarters

Rr Rug

Ss Sheep

Tt Turquoise

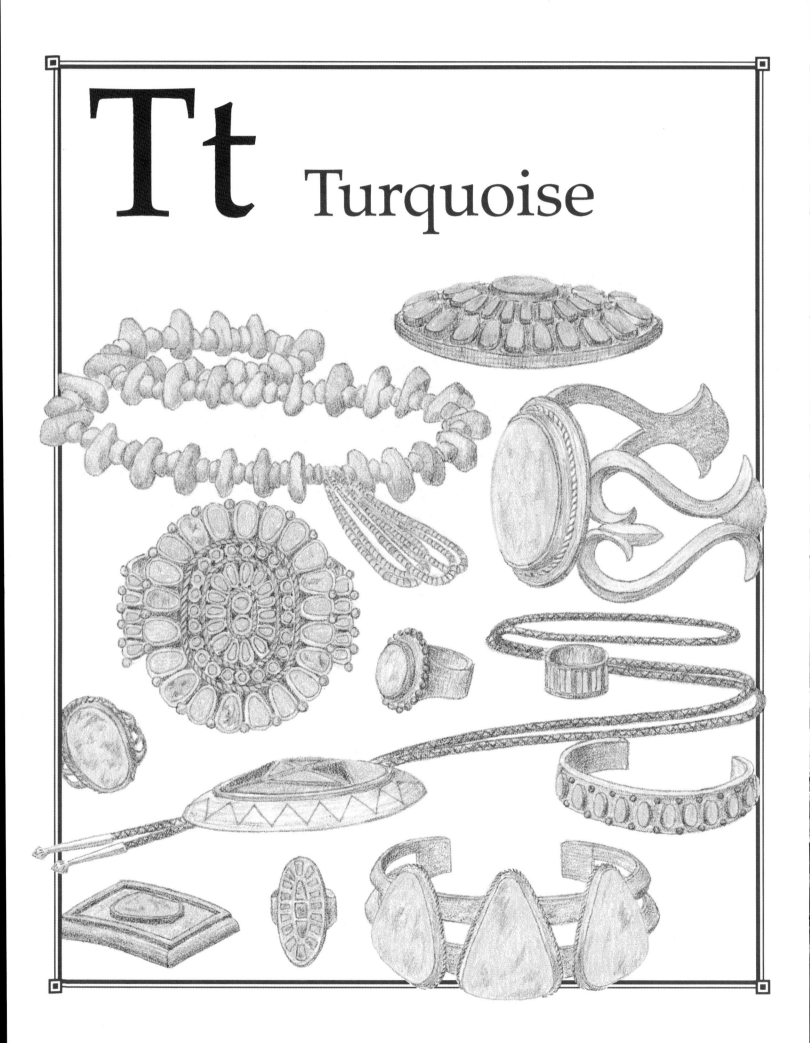

Uu Uncle

Vv Velvet

Ww Wedding basket

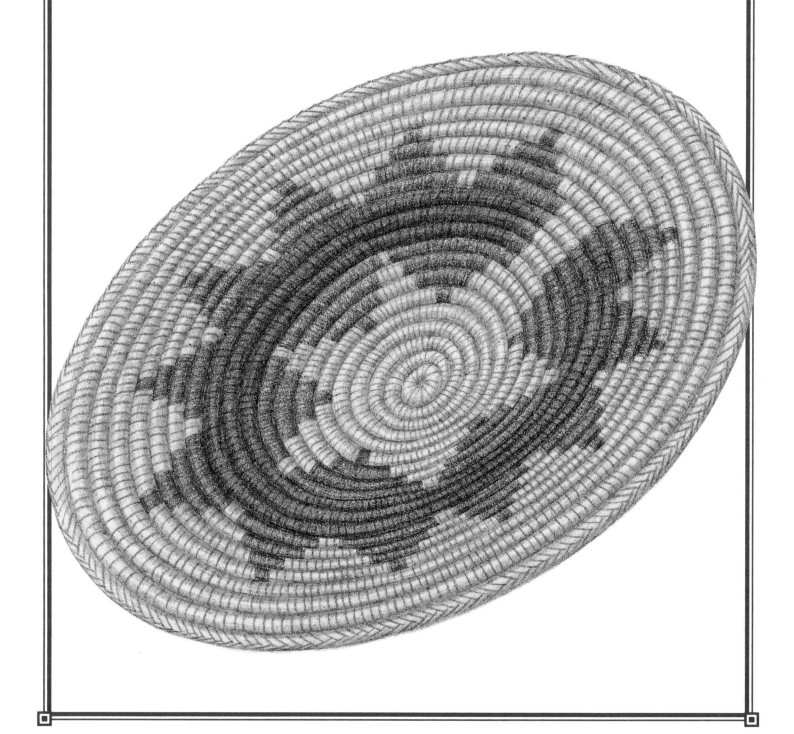

Xx X design

Yy Yucca

Zz Zas

About the pronunciation guide

The written Diné language is a phonetic language, meaning that the spoken word is pronounced very much the way it is written. There are many sounds in Diné that don't exist in the English language. For the benefit of our young readers, this pronunciation guide does not try to explain the diacritical marks; rather, we have tried to convey a close version of the word as it is spoken.

Glossary

Arroyo—A **bikooh** *(bĕ kō)* is carved in the desert sand by sudden summer rains.

Belt—The designs on the **sis** *(sĭs)* represent rain, mountains, and the sun.

Cradle board—The sky, rainbows, sunbeams, clouds, and lightning bolts are represented in the **awéé ts'áál** *(ā wĕ săăl)*. They help the baby grow strong and healthy.

Dress—A **biil** *(bēĕl)* is a traditional woven rug dress that is worn for special events.

Earrings—The turquoise beads in a **jaatł'óół** *(jāā thŏll)* stand for the man, and the white shell stands for the woman. Together they are beautiful.

Fry bread—**Dahdíníilghaazh** *(dă dēē nēĕl hăăsh)* is a puffy, round bread that is served at all meals.

Grandma—Grandmothers teach the children, tell them stories, and sing to them. The mother's mother is called **shimásání** *(shĕ mă săw nĕ)* and her father is called **shicheii** *(shĕ chāy)*. The father's parents are called **shinálí** *(shĕ knăl ĕ)*.

Hooghan *(hō wăn)*—This *home,* or female hooghan, is used mainly to live in. A male hooghan, which has a forked roof, is used for ceremonies.

'I'íí'á *(ă ēē ŭh)*—Each evening, the *sunset* tells us to eat, rest, bathe, and plan for the next day. The sun helps all things grow so that the world becomes more beautiful.

Juniper berries—**Dzidzé** *(sĭh zĭh)* are eaten raw, roasted, or ground and mixed into blue corn mush or blue corn bread. They also have healing powers.

Kéyah *(kāy yăh)*—Navajo *land* is surrounded by four sacred mountains: Huerfano Mountain, Mount Taylor, and the San Francisco and Blanca Peaks. They were placed there to watch over us and help us stay strong.

Loom—**Dah'iistł'ǫ** *(dăh ĭs glōw)*. Weaving is a gift from Spider Woman, a holy being who believes that women should help support their families.

Moccasin—**Kélchí** *(kĕl chēē)* means "red shoe." The top part is made of reddish-brown buckskin, and the bottom is made of cowhide.

Necklace—This **yoo'nímazí** *(yŏ nēē mŏs ēē)* is sterling silver and set with turquoise stones. People can tell we are Diné by our jewelry.

'Ooljéé' *(ōl jāā)*—The *moon* is sometimes called "a beautiful horse." Its brightness and beauty make people want to sing, tell stories, and visit one another. A full moon is called hanííbą́ą́z *(hă knēē băs)*, meaning "it has circled the world."

Pottery—The design around the top of the **'ásaa'** *(ăh săw)* is the "necklace" or "doorway." Each 'ásaa' has its own song and prayer.

Quarters—**Naaki yáál** *(năw kēȳ yăăl)*. When we first saw silver coins, we liked their beauty and began to use them as buttons and as decoration for our blouses.

Rug—**Diyogí** *(dĭ yŏ kēȳ)*. Diné women are famous for their beautiful **diyogí**. Women who weave bring honor to our people and our history.

Sheep—We have songs and prayers to give thanks for the **dibé** *(dĭh bĕ)* and to keep them healthy. Little children are given a lamb, a béhé *(bĕh hĕh)*, to take care of so they will become responsible.

Turquoise—**Dootł'izhii** *(dō t'li shēē)* represents Mount Taylor, a sacred mountain. Wearing turquoise gives us strength and good health.

Uncle—An uncle cares for and disciplines his nieces and nephews by telling stories and singing songs that teach. **Shidá'í** *(shĕ dăh ēē)* means the mother's brother, and **shibízhí** *(shĕ bēē shĕ)* means the father's brother.

Velvet—**Naak'a'at'ą́hí dishohígíí** *(năk ăh ĕtĕhĕ dēēshō kē ŭgēē)* is beautiful with our jewelry. From far away, the mountains look like they are draped with velvet.

Wedding basket—A **ts'aa'** *(t'săw)* is made from dried sumac. The colors represent the sacred mountains, the holy people, the sun, and the earth. A ts'aa' is needed for all ceremonies.

X design—**Naneeshtł'iizh** *(năw nēēsh lēēsh)*. Zigzag lines, X's, and triangles are traditional Diné designs. The colors stand for the four seasons and directions.

Yucca—**Tsá'ászi'ts'óóz** *(šeh ăh že ōs)* (soap yucca) is used as a shampoo and detergent after it is pounded and soaked in water. It is also used to cure certain illnesses.

Zas, or **Yas** *(zăhs)*—*Snow* is welcomed because it means a good spring planting season and food for the animals. Sometimes we wash in zas to build strength and prevent illness.